Auntie Francis and her Henchmen

By: Allison McWood

Annelid Press

AUNTIE FRANCIS AND HER HENCHMEN
Copyright © 2020 by Allison McWood.
FIRST EDITION

Cover Design by: Daniel Greenhalgh

ISBN: 978-1-7771360-4-8

Cast List

FRANCIS --An alcoholic

PETRA --- Her niece

ANGELA--- Petra's mother

BERNARD---Petra's brother

CLAY   --A distant cousin

LEGION ---An entity

MAMMON---An entity

ACT ONE, SCENE ONE

FRANCIS's kitchen. LEGION and MAMMON slink into the room, mumbling a series of unintelligible grunts. Each take a hiding place. A corpse is stiff in a kitchen chair at the breakfast table.

FRANCIS   *(from another room)* Sweetheart?...Honey, it's morning!...Is there something wrong? Why won't you answer? *(enters)* Are you up?...Honey? *(lights cigarette)* Some company would be nice. *(takes a bottle of rum out of the cupboard and embraces it)* There you are. Were you hiding from me? Love of my life. *(takes a swig)*

BERNARD   *(from another room)* Auntie Francis? Are you out of bed?

FRANCIS   In here, Bernard.

BERNARD   *(entering)* Morning, Auntie Francis. Do we have any cereal?...Something smells.

FRANCIS   *(pouring two bowls of cereal)* Did you sleep well, or does the basement still have that draft?

BERNARD   The draft isn't the problem. It's the grunting.

FRANCIS   *(pouring rum on the cereal)* Grunting?

BERNARD   Auntie Francis, that's rum.

FRANCIS   That one's mine. You take the other bowl. What grunting?

BERNARD   The basement grunts. If I knew why, I'd put a stop to it.

FRANCIS   *(picking up phone and dialing)* That's lovely.

BERNARD   Lovely? A grunting basement?

FRANCIS   *(into phone)* Mr. Flynn, please.

BERNARD   I'm dropping off my university application this morning. Do my eyes look puffy?

FRANCIS   *(covering receiver)* Bernard, haven't I always told you university is a sham? I'm uneducated. Do what I do. *(into phone)* Mr. Flynn? It's Francis. I won't be working today.

BERNARD   Again?

FRANCIS   *(into phone)* Because, Mr. Flynn, I am sick.

BERNARD   Auntie Francis...

FRANCIS   *(into phone)* I am a sick, sick, puppy.

BERNARD   I'll brew some coffee.

FRANCIS   *(into phone)* Good-bye, Mr. Flynn.

BERNARD   I want your life.

FRANCIS   Hmmm?

BERNARD   You haven't gone to work for seven months and they still send you a paycheck.

FRANCIS   They owe me. It's hard work banging all those senior executives.

BERNARD   Who's doing your job? What if they replace you?

FRANCIS   Replace me? You are so cute.

BERNARD   But...

FRANCIS   Bernard, you are not paying attention. *(taking a swig of rum in an unladylike pose, with a cigarette hanging out of her mouth)* I did not get where I am today with an education or whatever. I am wise. Not educated, but wise. There's a difference, you know.

BERNARD   So you're saying I should...

FRANCIS   There are two kinds of people in this world. Those who work, and those who are wise.

BERNARD   Excuse me?

FRANCIS   I'm here for the ride, Baby. As long as there are people who work hard, people like us can live the good life.

BERNARD   Us?

FRANCIS   You want to be like me, don't you?

BERNARD   Of course I do. You're wise.

FRANCIS   My boy.

BERNARD   *(ripping paper)* I suppose I have no use for this university application.

FRANCIS   There's a good lad. A life of freedom awaits you. Let's celebrate with this box of truffles. I think there's alcohol in them.

BERNARD   *(leaving)* Can you hold that thought for about a half an hour?

FRANCIS   A half an hour? But my short term memory doesn't stretch that far.

BERNARD   Mom needs me.

FRANCIS   Oh, poo.

BERNARD   She has that rare spleen disease. She phoned me last night and said it's acting up again. I thought I'd drive over and see if there's anything I can do.

FRANCIS   Angela. Urgh! She's always trying to take what's mine!

BERNARD   She's ill.

FRANCIS   She's possessed.

BERNARD   She's your sister.

FRANCIS   Angela. Ug! My lips can barely manipulate themselves around that name. Angela has demons seeping from her pores!

ANGELA   *(entering)* I brought a casserole!

FRANCIS   Angela! How wonderful!

ANGELA   The door was open. I hope you don't mind.

FRANCIS   A casserole.

ANGELA   Francis, I was thinking about you last night. You haven't been to work in a while, and I was worried. I was up all night cooking. I hope you like noodles.

BERNARD   You were up cooking all night? Mom, what about your rare spleen disease?

ANGELA   I took something for the pain and something else for the side-effects. That's not important. What's important is my little sister. *(pulling out a spoon)* It's comfort food. Here, Francis, let me feed you.

BERNARD   Mom, maybe you should go home and rest.

ANGELA   Bernard, I'm not important. I've told you that. We must always put others first.

BERNARD   But, Mom...

ANGELA   Francis! What are you doing on your feet? *(seating FRANCIS next to the corpse)* Rest here, Love...Do you smell something?

FRANCIS   Honestly, Angela, I don't know why you forced me against my will to move to the suburbs.

ANGELA   *(cringing for a moment in pain)* I'm not sure I know what you mean, dear.

FRANCIS   I enjoyed the city. The bars. The nightlife. All my friends were there.

                                    ANGELA feeds FRANCIS another spoonful.

ANGELA   I thought...

FRANCIS   You're confused. I moved here to look after you. Out of the goodness of my heart.

BERNARD   Didn't you just say you were forced against your will?

FRANCIS   Bernard, has your mother been confusing you again? Would you look at that, Angela. You are a bad influence on your son.

ANGELA   I'm sorry. I promise I...*(cringes)*

BERNARD   Mom, that's the second time you've cringed since you got here. Are you sure you're alright?

ANGELA   Don't worry about me. I deserve it.

FRANCIS   You certainly do. Jeez. The things you do for pity.

BERNARD   I'm calling Petra.

FRANCIS   You'll do no such thing.

ANGELA   She's studying, Bernie. She has exams.

BERNARD   I'll get Petra to bring over some medication.

FRANCIS   Put down that phone, you little cockroach!

ANGELA   Do as your auntie says.

BERNARD   What's the matter with you two?

FRANCIS   That hussy is not welcome in my home.

BERNARD   Who? Petra?

FRANCIS   I forbid you to talk to her.

BERNARD   I can try, but her being my sister may pose a problem.

FRANCIS   Petra is lazy. Immoral. Completely dim-witted.

ANGELA   She's my little girl.

FRANCIS   That explains it then.

BERNARD   You think Petra is dim-witted?

ANGELA   Listen to your auntie. She's wise.

FRANCIS   I remember when Petra was a baby. I didn't trust her.

BERNARD   You didn't trust a baby?

FRANCIS   Every time I picked her up, she peed on me. It was all part of her plan.

BERNARD   Plan?

FRANCIS   Do you remember Petra's first word?

ANGELA   Oh yes! It was onomatopoeia.

FRANCIS   She was always trying to make us look bad.

BERNARD   Auntie Francis, don't you think...

                                        ANGELA screams, noticing the corpse in the chair.

FRANCIS   What is it now, Angela?

ANGELA   It's, it's...oh! How horrible!

FRANCIS   Angela, please. You are being quite irritating.

ANGELA   It's Norbert! He's dead! Oh! He's dead!

BERNARD   Oh crap.

FRANCIS   Who's Norbert.

BERNARD   Your husband.

FRANCIS   Oh.

ANGELA   Norbert! Oh! He's gone! He's gone! Poor Norbert!

FRANCIS   Oh, Angela. There's no need to overreact.

CLAY   *(entering)* I've arrived.

BERNARD   Who are you?

CLAY   Cousin Clay.

BERNARD   We have a cousin Clay?

CLAY   Your Uncle Farley's boy.

BERNARD   We have an Uncle Farley?

CLAY   Uncle Farley. Portly gentleman. Mutton chops. Elbow patches on his jacket.

BERNARD   Where did you come from?

CLAY   Wyoming. Hopped on a plane the moment I heard the bad news about Uncle Norbert. That him, slumped in the chair?

BERNARD   We just discovered his body two minutes ago. How could you possibly...

CLAY   Brought a copy of the will.

FRANCIS   Give that to me.

BERNARD   How did you get a copy of Uncle Norbert's will?

CLAY   Norbert and I were like this. Notice how I'm crossing my middle finger with my pointy finger? That signifies how close we were.

FRANCIS   He never mentioned you.

CLAY   Auntie Francis, can I call you Auntie Francis? You have always been my favourite aunt.

FRANCIS   I like you.

CLAY   Thought you might. That's why I thought I might be of some comfort to you in this, your gravest hour. Did I say grave? Sorry about that. didn't mean to rub your nose in it. Now take a gander at that will. Go ahead. Read.

FRANCIS   My head gets a bit swimmy after I eat cereal. Could you read the will for me?

CLAY   Don't mind if I do. *(to ANGELA)* It's Amanda, isn't it?

ANGELA   Angela.

CLAY   Angela, why don't you go somewhere and grieve? It's hit us all hard. There you go.

ANGELA   I'll break the news to Petra. *(exits)*

CLAY   That's right. You go feed the cat.

FRANCIS   The will, Clay.

CLAY   That's why I'm here. I'll paraphrase if that's alright with the two of you. It seems the old troll is worth more now that he's dead. And when I say troll, I mean that in the fondest, possible way.

FRANCIS   How much did Norbert leave me?

CLAY   Everything.

FRANCIS   Now when you say everything...

CLAY   *(showing will)* Take a look at these numbers.

FRANCIS   *(looking at will)* Holy frig! I've never seen so many zeros in my life. Bernard...

BERNARD   Auntie Francis, are we rich?

FRANCIS   I can't believe this! I'll never have to work again!

BERNARD   How is that different from...

FRANCIS   At last! I can quit my job and sunbathe naked on the sands of Mexico! This is the best thing that has ever happened to me! Who wants rum? *(LEGION, hiding in the cupboard, hands FRANCIS a bottle)* Thank you.

BERNARD   Shouldn't we do something with Uncle Norbert?

FRANCIS   Let the dead bury themselves. *(pulls credit card from NORBERT'S pocket)* Let's celebrate. It's on Norbert.

BERNARD   Wouldn't this be an appropriate time to mourn?

FRANCIS	Stop being so morbid. Life is a party that doesn't stop. Now we can party in style. Norbert's treat.
BERNARD	Are you sure you're okay, Auntie Francis?
FRANCIS	I'm fine. I was going to leave him anyway. Norbert was such a control freak. Always trying to make me go thirsty. That reminds me. What beverages should we serve at the party?
BERNARD	I'll pick you up whatever you need at the liquor store.
CLAY	I'll get my suitcase.
FRANCIS	Suitcase?
CLAY	Family needs to stick together in times of sorrow. I'll be moving into your basement.
BERNARD	Wait a minute...
FRANCIS	I feel no sorrow.
CLAY	Let us rejoice together then.

> LEGION and MAMMON creep out from their hiding places and watch FRANCIS, BERNARD and CLAY, who are unaware that they are being watched.

ACT ONE, SCENE TWO

> *PETRA is in her bedroom, studying.*

PETRA   Stay awake, Petra.

> *Enter ANGELA.*

ANGELA   Oh good. You're not doing anything.

PETRA   I'm studying, Mom. I came home from a thirteen hour shift and now I'm studying.

ANGELA   Oh, Petra!

PETRA   Mom?

ANGELA   Uncle Norbert has gone home to be with Jesus!

PETRA   Uncle Norbert? What? Dead? This is devastating!

ANGELA   The party starts in twenty minutes. Get your things.

PETRA   Party?

ANGELA   I got a call on my cell phone on my way home. Francis is throwing a party with fine cuisine and expensive wines.

PETRA   I don't drink.

ANGELA   Petra, Auntie Francis just lost her husband.

PETRA   So why is she throwing a party?

ANGELA   She's grieving in her own way.

PETRA   I'm not going to a party. That's sick.

ANGELA   Your auntie needs you.

PETRA   She doesn't even like me.

ANGELA   Petra!

PETRA   How can Auntie Francis celebrate at a time like this? She's having a party and Uncle Norbert isn't going to be there.

ANGELA   I think he still might be in the kitchen.

PETRA   Forget it.

ANGELA   It'll be fun. Cousin Clay came all the way from Wyoming. You remember Cousin Clay.

PETRA   No.

ANGELA   I was hoping somebody did.

PETRA   I can't go over there. There's something about that house. Something...wrong.

ANGELA   But Auntie Francis needs...

PETRA   She says things to me.

ANGELA   What things?

PETRA   Things that hurt. Things that don't make any sense.

ANGELA   She drinks sometimes.

PETRA   Sometimes?

ANGELA   It's the alcohol talking. What she says doesn't count when she's drinking.

PETRA   I suppose if Auntie Francis got in a car and killed someone, that wouldn't count either.

ANGELA   You're being saucy.

PETRA   She has a problem.

ANGELA   Which is why we need to support her.

PETRA   In what?

ANGELA   We're the only family she has. We can't leave her alone. What if...

PETRA   There's going to be booze at this party, isn't there? And she'll be smoking. I'm deathly allergic to cigarette smoke.

ANGELA   Don't you love your Auntie Francis?

PETRA   That's not the issue. The woman has a problem and I seem to be the only one who sees it. Bernard lives in the woman's basement, for crying out loud.

ANGELA   He's being supportive. Bernard is a good boy.

PETRA   I'm studying.

ANGELA   She wouldn't hurt you if she knew what she was saying. She's your aunt.

PETRA   Then why doesn't she love me?

ANGELA   She...It's not as bad as you make it out to be.

PETRA   Mom, Auntie Francis is out of control.

ACT ONE, SCENE THREE

FRANCIS is alone in darkness.

FRANCIS   I have complete control.

Enter LEGION and MAMMON. They are slinking around FRANCIS, grunting unintelligibly.

FRANCIS   Where have you two been? A woman has needs, you know.

LEGION hands FRANCIS a bottle of rum and MAMMON lights a cigarette for FRANCIS.

FRANCIS   Things are finally going my way. No job to fence me in, no husband to push me around. I even have two slaves in my basement, posing as devoted nephews. And a sister who's too sick to do anything about it. Has a woman ever achieved this much power? *(puffs on cigarette)* But it's not easy being the centre of the universe. At any time the wind could shift and all this beautiful revelry will sift like sand through my fingers. *(pushing LEGION and MAMMON off her)* Make sure that doesn't happen. *(pulling dollar bills out of her pockets, throwing them at LEGION and MAMMON)* Take this and go to them.

BERNARD   *(from beyond darkness)* Auntie Francis?

FRANCIS   *(to LEGION and MAMMON)* What are you still doing here, you miserable pukes? Take this money and get out of here.

> *LEGION and MAMMON scurry out with the money.*

FRANCIS   I need a drink.

> *Lights come up. FRANCIS is in her kitchen. Enter BERNARD with a keg of whiskey around his neck. BERNARD does not see that LEGION is following closely behind. LEGION disappears after he dumps money all over the floor.*

BERNARD   I'm back.

FRANCIS   *(grabbing whiskey)* Bernard, you're a saint! *(guzzles)*

> *BERNARD notices money on the floor, picks it up and puts it in his pocket.*

BERNARD   You're still in your bathrobe. Aren't the guests going to be here soon?

FRANCIS   What would I do without my Bernard?

BERNARD   Aw.

> *Exit FRANCIS.*

> *BERNARD begins stocking the*

fridge with bottles of rum.

LEGION enters, slinking towards BERNARD. LEGION begins handing BERNARD the bottles of rum as he puts them in the fridge. BERNARD stiffens and looks around.

BERNARD   Is somebody here?

LEGION taps BERNARD on the shoulder. BERNARD turns around quickly.

BERNARD   Hello?

ANGELA   *(from the other room)* Hello?

BERNARD   Thank God.

Enter ANGELA and PETRA..

ANGELA   I brought angel food cake!

BERNARD   That's swell.

LEGION points at PETRA. BERNARD walks toward PETRA.

BERNARD   Hi, Petra.

BERNARD slaps PETRA.

Exit LEGION.

PETRA   What was that for?

BERNARD   You looked like you needed to be slapped.

PETRA   Mom!

ANGELA   I'm sure he had a good reason, dear.

BERNARD   Have either of you seen Cousin Clay?

>   *MAMMON enters, leading CLAY into the room by luring him with a wad of money. CLAY follows, sniffing the money, somewhat like a dog.*

BERNARD   Clay?

>   *MAMMON is startled and drops the money on the floor. He slithers out of the room. CLAY scrambles to pick the money up.*

BERNARD   Have you taken care of Uncle Norbert's affairs?

CLAY   I sold him to a laboratory.

BERNARD   Where's the money?

CLAY   Tied up in investments.

PETRA   I don't smell cigarette smoke and I don't hear ice cubes clinking. Does this mean Auntie Francis has decided not to show up?

ANGELA   Petra, I wish you would be more sensitive to your auntie's feelings. She's mourning. This is a very sorrowful time for her.

                                                    Enter FRANCIS, wearing a black, widow's dress and a black, wide-brimmed hat with a veil over her face.

FRANCIS   Look, everyone! I'm a widow!

ANGELA   You poor soul!

FRANCIS   Don't I look adorable in this outfit? And just to be festive, I brought sackcloth for everyone!

CLAY   Beautiful. When's dinner?

FRANCIS   *(taking dinner out of the oven)* I've prepared something extra special for all my loved ones.

PETRA   What is it?

FRANCIS   *(lights cigarette and puffs)* Lung.

BERNARD   Mmmmmm!

PETRA   Looks a bit charred, doesn't it? *(she goes into a coughing fit)*

FRANCIS	Would you knock off the coughing melodrama? We all know you don't really have a smoke allergy.

> *LEGION and MAMMON creep back. They cover the ears of ANGELA, BERNARD and CLAY.*

PETRA	*(coughing)* Right. Like I'm making this up.
FRANCIS	I suppose you're going to force me to extinguish my cigarette, even though this is my house.
PETRA	Could you, please?
FRANCIS	*(extinguishing)* Slut. Bloody non-smokers prancing around like they own the place.
PETRA	Auntie Francis, smoke makes it very difficult for me to breathe. I feel smothered whenever I'm around you.
FRANCIS	You have a pimple.
PETRA	What?
FRANCIS	Right there, on your chin. I thought everyone in the room might want to know.
PETRA	I don't see how that has anything to do with...
FRANCIS	Who wants to see Petra's pimple?
PETRA	What the...

FRANCIS   Not as perfect as you thought you were, eh, princess?

PETRA   Why are you doing this?

FRANCIS   Don't look so hurt. I'm only trying to help.

PETRA   Help?

FRANCIS   We can't have you thinking too highly of yourself. Pride is a sin, darling. It's not healthy.

PETRA   I...

FRANCIS   Let's open presents while we wait for the lung to harden.

CLAY   Presents?

FRANCIS   I have been blessed. The floodgates of heaven have been opened, and I want so much to share the bounty with my family. I even brought something for the slut.

PETRA   Why do you keep calling me that? I'm a virgin.

ANGELA   Petra! Such language!

                                    LEGION and MAMMON cover the eyes of BERNARD and CLAY.

FRANCIS   We all know about you, Petra.

PETRA   Would you mind telling me so I know too?

FRANCIS   Stop playing the ingenue. It's obvious to everyone that you are having adult relations with furniture.

PETRA   What?

BERNARD   I always suspected it.

CLAY   Tart.

PETRA   That makes absolutely no sense.

FRANCIS   I know what's been going on between you and my ottoman. It's disgusting, but I'm willing to overlook it because I'm your auntie and I love you.

PETRA   How could you possibly suggest...

FRANCIS   You must do something about your unnatural urges.

PETRA   I'm not the one who had an STD named after me.

FRANCIS   Hey! That was a very rare STD! Only Albinos contract it, and it's hardly worth mentioning!

PETRA   My point being...

FRANCIS   The point of a pervert is undoubtedly warped.

PETRA   Mom!

ANGELA   My little girl is chaste.

FRANCIS   And if you believe that, then you're just as naïve as

Petra is.

ANGELA   Francis! How could you suggest a thing like that
                about...*(LEGION* covers ANGELA'S *eyes)* Petra, please
                stop having sex with furniture.

CLAY   Did someone say something about presents?

FRANCIS   Absolutely. Inheritance is only meaningful if you can
                share it with your loved ones. Angela, I'm sending you
                to Fiji.

ANGELA   Oh, Francis!

FRANCIS   Some relaxation will be good for your health. Of
                course, you'll need your little sister to come along   to
                look after you.

ANGELA   How fun! I can cook your meals, massage your feet and
                serve you cocktails on the beach with those little
                umbrellas in them!

FRANCIS   I thought you might say that...Here, Bernard. *(hands
                him a captain's hat)*

BERNARD   A hat?

FRANCIS   A boat.

BERNARD   A b...Whoa! Like a schooner?

FRANCIS   A cruise-liner.

BERNARD   Holy frig!

FRANCIS   Only the best for my Bernard.

CLAY   Where's mine?

FRANCIS   He's in the backyard.

CLAY   He?

FRANCIS   I bought you an elephant.

CLAY   Is there a sentimental innuendo behind this gift?

FRANCIS   I just thought you might like an elephant.

CLAY   So you won't mind if I trade him in for cash.

FRANCIS   He's yours. Whatever you decide to do with him is fine
               with me...Petra.

PETRA   Why are you looking at me that way?

FRANCIS   Don't you want your gift?

PETRA   Are there strings?

FRANCIS   Sweetheart, I'm your auntie. Take it.

                              PETRA opens an envelope.

PETRA   This is five thousand dollars.

FRANCIS   Petra, I don't want you to worry about how you're
               going to pay for university.

PETRA   I thought you didn't lo...I didn't think you c...Is this for
               real?

FRANCIS   I care about you as much as I care about a good
               education. You deserve it.

PETRA   This is too generous. I can't accept this. There's no way
               I'd ever be able to pay you back.

FRANCIS   It's a gift. It's yours.

PETRA   I, um...I don't know what to say.

FRANCIS   Why don't you just give me a hug and say, "thank you,
               Auntie Francis?"

PETRA   Thank you, Auntie Francis.

FRANCIS   There's my girl.

CLAY   How come she got cash?

                              Fade   out   everyone   except
                              FRANCIS, LEGION and MAMMON.
                              FRANCIS   and   LEGION   are
                              waltzing.

FRANCIS   What a team we make. Happiness is almost mine. It's
               so close. So close. I don't know what it is I'm looking
               for, but I almost have it. And you will find it for me.

                              MAMMON hands FRANCIS a
                              bottle of rum and cuts in to dance
                              with LEGION.

FRANCIS   But there's still something missing. A cogwheel. A puzzle piece.

                                            LEGION and MAMMON grunt unintelligibly.

FRANCIS   You know something that I don't. What are you keeping from me?...Would you stop dancing and grunting and tell me what you know?

                                            LEGION and MAMMON continue to dance and grunt. FRANCIS pulls out a horsewhip and cracks it. Dancing stops abruptly.

FRANCIS   Listen, you couple of shadowy turds, let's get something straight. I am in control. I have always been in control. I hold the whip and I make the rules. Is that simple enough for you?

                                            LEGION and MAMMON grunt to each other.

FRANCIS   This isn't about you. It's all about me. Because I am the centre of the universe. The universe I have created for myself. But what are you hiding? You know what it is that's cramping my happiness. What secret are you hiding in your subliminal grunts?

                                            Grunting continues. FRANCIS cracks whip.

FRANCIS   Take care of it. Find the problem and fix it.

LEGION and MAMMON exit.

ACT ONE, SCENE FOUR

PETRA is studying in her bedroom. There is a knock at her door.

PETRA   Studying.

ANGELA   Bedtime, Sweetie.

PETRA   No time, Mom.

Enter ANGELA.

ANGELA   Oh, Petra, your eyes.

PETRA   Let me focus. I have to go to work in an hour.

ANGELA   Call in sick, Petra. Your eyes...

PETRA   I promised myself I wouldn't take out a student loan.

ANGELA   What about the five thousand dollars Auntie Francis gave you?

PETRA   I bought a textbook and the government took the rest.

ANGELA   Why do you do this to yourself?

PETRA   I'm so tired.

ANGELA   This is suicide, what you're doing.

PETRA   So tired.

ANGELA   We're worried about you, Petra. We love you.

PETRA   We?

ANGELA   Your family. Me. Bernard. Cousin Clay, whoever he is. Auntie Francis.

PETRA   Auntie Francis...Mom, why did Auntie Francis give me that money? I always thought she hated me.

ANGELA   Family is all we have. Even when everything crumbles around us like stale cookies, family is...

PETRA   I thought she hated me. But when she gave me that money, it was like her way of saying...

ANGELA   She loves you. Turn your light out and think about that.

                                           Exit ANGELA. PETRA continues
                                           studying. She dozes off, falling
                                           asleep on her books. The voice of
                                           FRANCIS speaks to her in her
                                           sleep, while LEGION and
                                           MAMMON creep out from their
                                           hiding places. PETRA writhes
                                           around in her sleep, as the voice
                                           of FRANCIS haunts her.

FRANCIS   *(a voice)* You're lazy. Do you hear me, Petra? Lazy. You're a spoiled brat. Lazy sluggard. Brat. You're lazy. When will you grow up? Lazy, Petra. Lazy.

PETRA   *(groggily)* No, Auntie Francis. You love me.

                                        LEGION and MAMMON skulk
                                        around PETRA.

FRANCIS   Do you remember the first thing I ever said to you
               when you were a baby, Petra?

PETRA   No!

FRANCIS   You remember.

PETRA   I'm lazy.

FRANCIS   I looked into your crib and said, "Petra, you are lazy."

PETRA   I was just a...

FRANCIS   You were a lazy little scab, lying in your crib. Always
               expecting others to do everything for you.

PETRA   No!

FRANCIS   Lazy.

PETRA   No!

FRANCIS   You're lazy, Petra.

PETRA   No!

FRANCIS   I've always told you that. Haven't I always told you
               that?

PETRA   Stop it! I'm not! I'm not! What do I have to do to prove...*(awakens abruptly)* I was sleeping. What was I doing sleeping? I have exams.

PETRA continues studying. LEGION and MAMMON creep around her. PETRA suddenly becomes aware that there is a presence in her room. She stops what she is doing abruptly.

PETRA   Who's there?

MAMMON overturns PETRA'S school books, grabbing PETRA'S attention. PETRA gasps.

PETRA   Who are you?

LEGION and MAMMON slink closer and grunt unintelligibly.

PETRA   What do you want?

LEGION and MAMMON point at PETRA.

PETRA   Me? You can't have me. No, you can't. I'll scream for Mom. I'll phone Bernard. I...I'll...

LEGION grabs a framed picture from PETRA'S bedside table.

PETRA   What are you doing with that portrait? You can't have that!

LEGION grunts.

PETRA   That's my family! Give it to me, you son of a...

LEGION smashes the portrait.

ACT ONE, SCENE FIVE

FRANCIS's kitchen. BERNARD is wearing his captain's cap while steering an invisible boat. CLAY is counting money at the kitchen table.

BERNARD   Woo! Auntie Francis! She is like the Elvis of aunts. I could totally get used to this!

CLAY   There's a quality to the woman I find endearing.

BERNARD   All this gourmet food she's been stuffing us with.

CLAY   Mmmm. Expensive.

BERNARD   And the gifts.

CLAY   Lots of gifts.

BERNARD   I could only dream of living her life. She has such freedom.

CLAY   And generosity.

BERNARD   Independence.

CLAY   Discriminating taste.

BERNARD   Individuality.

CLAY   A palate for fine cuisine.

BERNARD	Passion.
CLAY	Loving nephews.
BERNARD	Wisdom.
CLAY	Money coming out her butt-crack.
BERNARD	Clay, do you ever ponder how lucky we are to have Auntie Francis?
CLAY	That I do, Cuz.
BERNARD	What did we do to deserve such a sainted aunt?
CLAY	How little you understand family. It's not about who deserves what. It's about togetherness. Auntie F is grateful for our companionship, and we are grateful for her bags of money. We're merely appreciating each other, as families ought to. It's all relative. Excuse the pun.
BERNARD	Speaking of family.
CLAY	Hmmm?
BERNARD	Where were you before Uncle Norbert died?
CLAY	That's not the point. I showed up when it counted and I'm staying right here with Auntie F until her pain subsides. Family's what matters, Cuz. Fam-il-y. Those are the three magic words. Wild buffalo couldn't drag me from my auntie in her time of need.

Enter FRANCIS.

FRANCIS   I'm broke.

CLAY   I'll be leaving now.

Exit CLAY.

BERNARD   Broke?

FRANCIS   Broke.

BERNARD   How is that possible? Uncle Norbert left you more money than a human being could spend in three lifetimes.

FRANCIS   The cheap bastard set up my inheritance so I'm issued funds monthly in measley, eighteen thousand dollar installments.

BERNARD   What happened to this month's money?

FRANCIS   It's in the wine cellar.

BERNARD   All of it?

FRANCIS   Not all of it. I was also nice enough to buy gifts for the family and for the slut.

BERNARD   How are we going to eat?

FRANCIS   What do you mean, eat? Priorities, Bernard.

BERNARD   Priorities?

FRANCIS   How am I going to throw a lavish party for myself with a limited cash flow?

BERNARD   Another party? I like the way your mind works.

Enter PETRA.

PETRA   There you are, Bernard. Mom's sick. We need you at home. Hello, Auntie Francis.

FRANCIS   This is his home, you little imp.

PETRA   Imp? What just happened? I thought when you gave me that money...

FRANCIS   Gave? What do you mean, gave?

PETRA   Um, the money. You know. The gift?

FRANCIS   You depraved little whore!

PETRA   Um, what?

FRANCIS   I gave you no money. You took it from me!

PETRA   I don't understand.

FRANCIS   How could you take advantage of a poor widow? Hold me, Bernard.

BERNARD   We'll get through this together, Auntie.

PETRA   Could someone please tell me what's going on?

FRANCIS   Give it back.

PETRA   Excuse me?

FRANCIS   The money. All of it.

PETRA   It's gone. I used it for school.

FRANCIS   You spent my money? Did you hear that, Bernard? Petra spent the last nickel of a grieving widow, surviving on a fixed income.

BERNARD   That was rather unsavoury.

PETRA   Unsavo...Bernard!

FRANCIS   You're standing rather close to that table, don't you think, Petra?

PETRA   Not the furniture thing again. *(sits in chair)*

FRANCIS   *(as PETRA sits)* Ah! That feels good!

PETRA   Now cut that out!

FRANCIS   Why don't you just take my end tables into the broom closet and have an orgy?

PETRA   I do not have romantic feelings for furniture!

FRANCIS   Oh, of course not. You're perfect in every way.

PETRA   I'm leaving.

FRANCIS   Not until you give me my money.

PETRA   I'm a student. You're asking a student for five thousand dollars.

FRANCIS   Students are supposed to be poor. That's why they call them poor students. Wealthy heiresses are supposed to be rich.

PETRA   You just said you were a poor widow.

BERNARD   Petra, give the money back to Auntie Francis. It's the right thing to do.

PETRA   What the...

BERNARD   It was never really yours.

FRANCIS   My boy.

PETRA   I don't see Auntie Francis going after you to get the cruise-liner back.

BERNARD   That is entirely different.

PETRA   How?

FRANCIS   That is money spent. The boat's been used and I can't return it. You, on the other hand, were issued cash. It would be in my pocket now if you hadn't spent it on frivolities.

PETRA   My education?

FRANCIS   Wasted on a simple mind.

PETRA   A simple mi...I'm on the Dean's list. My grade point average is...Oh, skip it. There's no use having a battle of wits with an unarmed woman.

BERNARD   Petra!

                              LEGION sneaks in and covers BERNARD'S eyes.

PETRA   Auntie Francis has a problem. Am I the only one who sees it?

BERNARD   I don't see a problem.

FRANCIS   That's because there isn't one. The only problem here is just about to leave. Isn't that right, Petra?

PETRA   You need help, Auntie Francis...And so do you, Bernard.

FRANCIS   Sweetness, that's ever so nice of you to be concerned for Auntie. But I'm afraid you're the one who needs help. Would you like me to skim through the yellow pages to find a nice therapist for you?

PETRA   Why can't you see...

FRANCIS   Please don't suck us into your delusions. Bernard and I are quite happy with reality the way it is.

PETRA   But...

FRANCIS   And don't let money come between family. Be a good girl and bring Auntie her money. It would be such a shame for you to break up the family with your pig-headedness.

PETRA   You...have a problem.

Exit PETRA.

BERNARD   *(with eyes still covered)* What problem does she mean, Auntie Francis?

ACT ONE, SCENE SIX

ANGELA is lying on a couch. She is weak and in a tremendous amount of pain. She reaches for the telephone and dials.

ANGELA   Hello? Is this the soup kitchen?...I am so sorry, but I'm not well enough to volunteer today... Forgive me. *(hangs up and looks at ceiling)* Forgive me.

Enter PETRA.

PETRA   She's done it again.

ANGELA   I'm sorry.

PETRA   Would you believe Auntie Francis is coming after me for five thousand dollars?

ANGELA   But you're just a student.

PETRA   That's what I said to her. Where am I going to come up with that kind of cash? I'm making minimum wage for the love of...

ANGELA   I am so sorry.

PETRA   Bernard says I should give it back.

ANGELA   No, no, Petra. That money was a gift.

PETRA   I shouldn't give it back? Now I'm confused.

ANGELA	I'm sorry.
PETRA	Sorry? Mom, why do you keep apologi...*(interrupted when ANGELA begins weeping)* Mom?
ANGELA	What kind of a human being am I? I just told the soup kitchen I couldn't...I couldn't...Oh, all those hungry people!
PETRA	Let me get you some tea.
ANGELA	Sit. You work too hard.
PETRA	Mom...
ANGELA	I wanted to work in the soup kitchen today. I meant to. But I guess I overdid it this morning. I wore myself out.
PETRA	What now?
ANGELA	I couldn't help myself. I saw a skinny prostitute shivering on a street corner. I felt bad for the poor thing. So I prepared her a rump roast and knit her an entire wardrobe of appropriate clothing.
PETRA	Mother, your spleen!
ANGELA	She was so skinny! And so are you. Wait here. I'll go make you a lasagna.
PETRA	Sit down, Mother.
ANGELA	I'm useless.

PETRA   You're not...

ANGELA   Completely useless.

PETRA   Mom...

ANGELA   Look at me! I never feel well. I can't even get off this couch. I'm a horrible mother. A horrible sister. A horrible...I don't know. Person?

PETRA   Mom, you just fed a starving prostitute.

ANGELA   I'm useless.

PETRA   Mother, you are not useless.

ANGELA   I'm a useless piece of poo.

PETRA   Why do you think that? Who put that in your head?

Enter FRANCIS.

FRANCIS   Angela, you're useless.

PETRA   What are you doing here?

FRANCIS   I thought the two of you might like some cigarette smoke blown in your faces.

PETRA   Mom's not up to visitors. She's not feeling well.

FRANCIS   Angela, you're a horrible mother. Would you take a look at this brat you've reared? She's beastly.

PETRA   Here we go.

FRANCIS   Petra has taken advantage of a poor widow. Were you
                 aware of that?

                               *LEGION and MAMMON skulk in.
                               They pull out some lawn chairs
                               and sit to watch.*

ANGELA   But she's just a student.

FRANCIS   The money is mine. I earned it. The little miser isn't
                 planning on giving it back to me.

PETRA   I never said that.

ANGELA   Petra, you're not honestly thinking of...

PETRA   I don't know. I don't know what to do. I'm confused.

FRANCIS   See! I told you she wouldn't give it back.

                               Enter BERNARD.

BERNARD   So this is where everyone has gotten to.

FRANCIS   Here's Bernard. Bernard, tell Angela about the money.

BERNARD   Petra's giving it back.

PETRA   Bernard!

                               LEGION and MAMMON share a

large bowl of popcorn as they watch.

ANGELA   Francis, you can't just give her a gift and…

FRANCIS   It wasn't a gift.

PETRA   I said…

BERNARD   Last I heard, Petra was giving the money back.

PETRA   I…

FRANCIS   She never said that. She said she was keeping it.

ANGELA   I never heard her say…

BERNARD   The money belongs to Auntie Francis.

ANGELA   Not after she gave it away.

PETRA   May I…

FRANCIS   I want my money.

ANGELA   Petra is not giving it back.

FRANCIS   Because she's selfish.

PETRA   But…

Enter CLAY.

CLAY   May I make an observation?

PETRA   Where did you come from?

CLAY   Petra is a hypocrite.

PETRA   I'm a hypocrite now?

CLAY   Petra has practically cut off Auntie Francis entirely. Yet she has no objections to taking her money.

ANGELA   She did not take...

FRANCIS   Shut up, Angela.

PETRA   I'm leaving.

Exit PETRA.

CLAY   Now take Bernard and I for example. Not once did we turn our backs on Auntie F.

BERNARD   Clay's right. Petra is so mean to Auntie Francis.

FRANCIS   And she violated my dinette set.

ANGELA   I don't believe it.

FRANCIS   You're blind.

CLAY   Bernard and I are entitled to...

BERNARD   What do you mean, "Bernard and I?" You just showed up yesterday.

CLAY   I've never trusted Petra.

BERNARD   Don't change the subject, Clay.

FRANCIS   Nearly everyone in this room senses a fishiness about Petra. Why can't you see that, Angela?

ANGELA   I'm not feeling well. Could you all just...

BERNARD   There you go with the guilt again. I don't need this.

FRANCIS   None of us do.

CLAY   I'd like to make another observation.

FRANCIS   Angela, you'd better change your attitude before our trip to Fiji.

ANGELA   We're not going to Fiji.

FRANCIS   What do you mean?

ANGELA   I gave our tickets away to some homeless people.

FRANCIS   How could you be so selfish?

ANGELA   Doing nice things for others cheers me up when I'm feeling rotten.

FRANCIS   Oh, stop. What do you have to feel rotten about?

BERNARD	Mom, you're out of control.
ANGELA	I wanted to help someone in need.
FRANCIS	What about my needs? What about your sister?
BERNARD	This whole family is out of control.
CLAY	It's Petra's fault.
FRANCIS	Ah! Finally, someone around here is making sense.
CLAY	Now about the money...
BERNARD	Forget about it, Clay. I'm her favourite nephew.
CLAY	Since when?
BERNARD	Here's a quarter. Buy yourself a clue.
CLAY	Hey, I flew in all the way from the Wyoming the minute I heard Auntie F was in distress.
BERNARD	Auntie Francis!
FRANCIS	Would you look at this, Angela? Your daughter is breaking up the family.

LEGION and MAMMON stand up and applaud.

ACT ONE, SCENE SEVEN

PETRA is studying in her bedroom.

PETRA   *(writing)* <u>Timon of Athens</u>, by William Shakespeare. Study question number one. Why did Timon rip off his clothes, leave his hair unscissored, live in a cave and become a misanthrope?...Maybe he had an Auntie Francis...Study question number two. Is it possible for a man of infinite wealth to bankrupt himself?...I am so confused.

Enter LEGION and MAMMON.

PETRA   Nothing makes sense anymore. The money's a gift, the money's not a gift. I'm keeping the money, I'm not keeping the money. I'm a prude but I'm humping the couch. I work myself into a coma but I'm a lazy sod. They're crazy, I'm crazy. They're deaf and I'm dumb. Francis grabs but I'm greedy. Francis drinks but I'm hallucinating. Francis infests but I get exterminated. My world is closing in on me and who in the heck is Cousin Clay?

LEGION and MAMMON grunt. PETRA turns around, startled.

PETRA   Where did you come from?

LEGION and MAMMON walk towards PETRA.

PETRA   Why won't you leave me alone? What did I do to provoke you?

> *LEGION and MAMMON close in on PETRA.*

PETRA
You have the wrong woman. I'm not the one with the problem. I'm no use to you. Auntie Francis is the one you want. Why do you keep coming after me?

> *LEGION grabs PETRA and pins her up against the wall.*

PETRA
You can't break me! Do you understand? I am educated! I'm a highly competent woman with goals and honours standing and...and goals. And education. I'm strong. I'm smart and highly motivated...So why do I feel so helpless?

> *LEGION gives PETRA a threatening shake, moving his face close to hers.*

PETRA
Who...who sent you?

LEGION
(raspy voice, slithering from his throat) Fran-cissss.

ACT TWO, SCENE ONE

ANGELA is in her kitchen, baking.
PETRA is with her.

ANGELA Auntie Francis is not out to get you.

PETRA I don't think you understand.

ANGELA She's sick, honey. It's the booze.

PETRA Mom, I really don't think you…

ANGELA She loves you. She was nice enough to invite you to the family Christmas dinner at her house.

PETRA Isn't family invited by default?

ANGELA *(chuckling)* Oh, Petra.

PETRA I'm not going.

ANGELA Not going to Christmas dinner?

PETRA Not if it's at her house.

ANGELA But Christmas is a happy time.

PETRA Your sister is a drunk.

ANGELA But I baked reindeer cookies.

PETRA   That doesn't change the fact that...

ANGELA   Couldn't you put your opinion aside for one day in the year?

PETRA   Auntie Francis is a drunk. That isn't an opinion, that's a fact. I can back it up.

ANGELA   Honestly, Sweetheart. Ever since you've been in university, you've been talking like an essay.

PETRA   We have a serious problem here.

ANGELA   There are no problems at Christmas.

PETRA   She's still a drunk.

ANGELA   Not at Christmas time.

PETRA   She's a drunk with cranberry sauce, then.

ANGELA   Petra, please. You're ruining Christmas.

PETRA   *I'm* ruining Christmas?

ANGELA   Don't you understand? Christmas is a time when...

PETRA   When we play carols really loud so we can't hear Auntie pop the cork?

ANGELA   Don't you love your auntie?

PETRA   Why do you have to ask me things like that?

ANGELA   Do you?

PETRA   She's a queeziness that I want to puke out, but can't.

ANGELA   Oh, Petra.

PETRA   She's a dry heave.

ANGELA   You don't love your auntie.

PETRA   I never said that.

ANGELA   You called her a dry heave.

PETRA   That's not the same as saying…

ANGELA   I don't want to think about things like this. Not when the stockings are hung.

PETRA   Do you think if we leave Santa some milk and cookies, he'll bring Auntie Francis some sobriety?

ANGELA   It's worth a try.

PETRA   Mother, pay attention. Auntie Francis is going to die if we don't…

ANGELA   Do you want to lick the egg-beater?

PETRA   It's not just a problem anymore, Mom. It's…it's alive now. These…I don't know…things…These things came into my bedroom and…

ANGELA   Where did I put those sprinkles?

PETRA   Have you ever seen the things, Mom? Or am I the only one who can see them?

ANGELA   Sprinkles, sprinkles.

PETRA   They're black things. Like shadows. Not people, so much as entities. Mom, am I losing it?

ANGELA   Most likely, dear. Try some pudding.

PETRA   I don't want pudding. I want an aunt.

ANGELA   You have one. You just don't love her.

PETRA   Why do you keep saying...

ANGELA   You say nasty things about her.

PETRA   She's left me with open sores. You have to expect some pus to come out.

ANGELA   You didn't know her before. Long ago before she started drinking. She was twelve then.

PETRA   Mom, I'm not saying...

ANGELA   Somewhere, deep, deep below the surface, Francis is still *little* Francis. My little sister. I can see it. Look deep, Petra. Maybe you can see it too. She's such a lovely person.

PETRA   Lovely person?

ANGELA   Remember when she gave you that money for school?
               That was the *real* Francis. That's the Francis I
               remember. We were little girls together. What fun we
               used to have.

PETRA   She's a stranger. I have no idea who my aunt is. Not
               even one sober memory do I have of her. Not one.

ANGELA   She can drink poison and puff on toxic fumes, and still
               she's as strong as an ox. She's so much stronger than I
               am. I wish...

PETRA   Don't even say it.

ANGELA   What do you have against Auntie Francis?

PETRA   Against her? Mom, she's everywhere. Like a stale fart. I
               can't escape. She's at every family gathering. She
               phones us every single day. My brother lives in her
               basement. You put her picture all around the house
               like a shrine to the Virgin Mother.

ANGELA   Petra...

PETRA   Everywhere I look, she's there. And there. And there.
               Even when she's not around I can hear her ice cubes
               clinking. I can hear her voice. But it's not *her* voice.
               When she talks, her lips move, but I swear someone
               else's voice is coming out.

ANGELA   Petra...

PETRA   Now she's sending those Things after me.

ANGELA   Stop it.

PETRA   I can't take it anymore. I wish she was...

ANGELA   Stop it!

PETRA   I wish she was...sober.

ANGELA   Why don't you love my little sister?

PETRA   If I didn't love her, I wouldn't care what she thought of me.

ANGELA   Do you love her?

PETRA   She's my aunt.

ANGELA   Do you?

ACT TWO, SCENE TWO

> *FRANCIS is in her kitchen with BERNARD and CLAY. She is feeding them puppy treats throughout the scene. Each time she feeds them a treat, they sit up and beg like dogs.*

FRANCIS   Is the turkey stuffed?

BERNARD   Did it.

FRANCIS   The tree trimmed?

CLAY   Done.

FRANCIS   What about the egg nog?

BERNARD   In the fridge.

CLAY   Anything else we should do for you, Auntie F?

FRANCIS   One thing.

BERNARD   Name it. Anything.

FRANCIS   Do something about Petra.

BERNARD   *Do* something?

FRANCIS   I love her. Like my own daughter. But it breaks my heart to see her rip the family apart. You know how important family is to me.

BERNARD   You're a loving heart, dear Auntie.

FRANCIS   I'm afraid she might do something to ruin Christmas. I considered not inviting her, but couldn't stand the idea of Petra not being here with us during the holidays.

CLAY   That is so like you.

FRANCIS   What I'm asking you to do is messy. Petra is unruly. She needs a good flogging.

CLAY   Not a problem, Auntie F.

FRANCIS   You can understand why I can't do the dirty work myself.

BERNARD   You are a caring and genuine aunt, who is incapable of being cruel.

FRANCIS   Exactly. Tough love is what Petra needs. It simply won't come from me.

BERNARD   What would you like us to do?

FRANCIS   Destroy her.

BERNARD   Destroy her?

FRANCIS   Tough love, Bernard.

BERNARD   But she's my sister.

CLAY
: I'll destroy her. I don't mind, really. I don't know her that well.

BERNARD
: But...

FRANCIS
: Who takes care of you?

BERNARD
: You do, Auntie Francis.

FRANCIS
: Does Petra love you as much as I do?

BERNARD
: Yes?

FRANCIS
: No.

BERNARD
: No.

CLAY
: Stupid. Auntie F loves us more than anyone. That's why she gives us things.

FRANCIS
: What has Petra done for you? I am your home. Your life jacket. Your guardian angel.

CLAY
: Your benefactor.

FRANCIS
: What kind of example is Petra anyway? Do you want to be like her? Do you want to work like a mule and still be broke?

BERNARD
: I want to be like you. I want to be on a perpetual, paid vacation.

FRANCIS
: Yes, my boy. We've figured out the system.

ANGELA   *(from next room)* Merry Christmas!

FRANCIS   You know what to do.

                                    Enter ANGELA and PETRA.

ANGELA   I brought a holiday, raisin cake.

PETRA   And here's the pudding. Maybe I should go now.

FRANCIS   Sweetness! Come hither and join in the festivities.

PETRA   I'm not sure I'm welcome.

FRANCIS   Angela, what have you been telling her?

ANGELA   I...

FRANCIS   Don't push me away, Petra dear. Auntie loves you. And so does everyone here.

BERNARD   Are you going to scarf up the five G's?

FRANCIS   Bernard, I thought I explained that I was going to be gracious about that matter. Petra may keep my money. I am a good aunt.

PETRA   Where should I put Bernard's present?

BERNARD   Keep it.

FRANCIS   What Bernard means to say is that your thoughtful gift is much too generous. He doesn't want you to starve.

Isn't that right, Bernard?

BERNARD   I don't want Petra's gift. I don't want to have anything to do with her.

FRANCIS   Bernard, this is a holy day. Let's forget about Petra's mistakes. We are about to sup together.

ANGELA   Set an extra place. I've invited a guest.

FRANCIS   You've invited a *what?*

ANGELA   His name is Bob. I found him panhandling outside the pastry shop.

FRANCIS   Bob?

ANGELA   He wasn't wearing shoes. I asked him if he had any family and he said no.

FRANCIS   Bob-with-no-shoes is not sitting at my table.

ANGELA   You'll get used to the smell.

FRANCIS   Christmas is for family. Bob is not family.

ANGELA   Bob has no family.

FRANCIS   You have completely missed the point of Christmas.

ANGELA   I was only trying to help. Helping others makes me feel better.

FRANCIS   Feel better about what? About being a lousy mother?

ANGELA   I'm sorry.

PETRA   You apologize to my mother!

ANGELA   No, Petra. Auntie is right.

FRANCIS   Who looks after your children while you're at home, popping pills?

PETRA   Mom's sick, you insensitive buzzard.

BERNARD   Remember who's house you're in, Petra.

ANGELA   I only wanted to...I was trying...

FRANCIS   Christmas or not, we don't need you disrupting the family, Angela. You are a depraved woman.

ANGELA   I'm sorry...I...Excuse me. I need to go clothe some orphans.

                            Exit ANGELA.

BERNARD   Who wants drinks?

PETRA   Bernard! What about Mom?

FRANCIS   Leave her. She'll be back when she smells my turkey.

BERNARD   What can I offer you, Auntie Francis?

FRANCIS   Some rum would be nice.

                                 BERNARD opens the fridge and takes out a revolver, handing it to FRANCIS.

FRANCIS   This is just what I need.

                                 FRANCIS takes the revolver and points it at her head.

PETRA   Auntie Francis! NO!

                                 PETRA tackles FRANCIS to the floor, trying to grab the revolver. When FRANCIS scrambles to her feet, she does not have a revolver in her hand. It is a bottle of rum.

FRANCIS   Are you possessed?

PETRA   You had a...I thought...I thought...I...This is rum.

FRANCIS   What else would it be?

PETRA   Bernard, what were you thinking? Handing an alcoholic a bottle of rum?

FRANCIS   Alcoholic?

BERNARD   Petra, stop making up stories.

                                 PETRA grabs rum from FRANCIS.

PETRA   You're killing yourself with this! You might as well be swallowing broken glass!

PETRA smashes bottle.

FRANCIS   You beast!

BERNARD   Who do you think you are, telling your aunt what she can drink? She's an adult!

PETRA   She's an adult who's slowly murdering herself, and I seem to be the only one who cares!

BERNARD   You don't care.

PETRA   I don't want to love her, but I do! Okay, there. I said it. I love Auntie Francis and I don't want her to die!

BERNARD   She's an adult!

PETRA   She's out of control!

FRANCIS   Who's out of control? *You* attacked *me,* I'm afraid.

PETRA   You have a problem.

FRANCIS   I don't have a...

PETRA   Can you go even one day without having a drink?

FRANCIS   As a matter of fact, there were twelve, consecutive years during which time I did not have a drink.

PETRA   The first twelve years of your life don't count.

FRANCIS   Baby, Love. Thank you for your concern. But there is no problem. I enjoy my life. How can there be a problem when I am so abnormally happy?

PETRA   You're out of...

FRANCIS   I have everything under control, okay? I am in control. I promise you.

BERNARD   She's an adult and this is her house.

PETRA   Bernard's right. An adult cannot be stopped from killing herself. Especially not in her own house.

FRANCIS   Thank you.

PETRA   But I'm not going to watch you do it.

FRANCIS   You're weird.

PETRA   I'm leaving and I'm not coming back until Auntie Francis gets help.

FRANCIS   You think you're so perfect. Trotting around, pointing out everyone's vices. You've never done anything wrong in your life, have you?

PETRA   I am not perfect. You remind me of that everyday.

FRANCIS   How perfect of you to say so.

PETRA   You're sick.

                        Exit PETRA.

FRANCIS   *(throwing something at the door)* There was only one person in the history of the world who was perfect! And they hung him on a cross!

CLAY   Would this be an inappropriate time to open presents?

ACT TWO, SCENE THREE

> *ANGELA is alone in her house, hugging a teddy bear.*

ANGELA She's my little sister. I need to look after her. She depends on me. Without me she'll...Francis loves me. I think. She's my little sister who needs me. She's my little...Why is she my little sister? Why do I have to love...why? Of all the sisters in the world, why *her*? Why? When I was in the hospital, hooked up to all those machines, why wasn't she beside me?

> *Fade in FRANCIS at the other end of the stage. Spot lit, she takes a drink.*

ANGELA Where was she? When did this happen to her? Where did she go?

> *LEGION and MAMMON carry FRANCIS offstage.*

> *PETRA appears in the doorway.*

ANGELA Make it stop hurting.

PETRA I'll get your medication.

ANGELA I don't have anything left.

PETRA Is the pharmacy open? I can get you some more.

ANGELA   She's taken it all.

PETRA   Who?

ANGELA   Francis has turned my family against me.

PETRA   Mom...

ANGELA   My only nephew thinks I'm the enemy. And Francis has taken my children away.

PETRA   What about me?

ANGELA   They're not her children. They're mine.

PETRA   What about...

ANGELA   What's happened to Bernard? How could he turn on the one who made him peanut butter sandwiches and powdered his little bum?

PETRA   I...

ANGELA   My own children love my drunk sister more than their own mother.

PETRA   Would you pay attention? I have not deserted you. I am immune to Auntie Francis and her inane puppeteering. There is no way she can beckon me to her basement.

ANGELA   Yes, but you have sex with furniture.

PETRA   I do not.

ANGELA   You don't?

PETRA   For the love of...Mother. Furniture?

ANGELA   But Francis said...

PETRA   Mom, the woman's down to one brain cell.

> *LEGION and MAMMON sneak into the room.*

ANGELA   Would my sister lie to me?

PETRA   She doesn't even know she's lying. It's creepy.

ANGELA   But Francis wouldn't...It must be the spirits.

> *LEGION and MAMMON run offstage.*

PETRA   The what?

ANGELA   The booze. The alcohol?

PETRA   Right.

ANGELA   I know she doesn't mean it. So why does it still hurt? And Bernard...

PETRA   I'll handle Bernard.

ANGELA   When you say *handle*...

PETRA   Mom, let me take care of this.

ANGELA   Promise me you won't say something that will...

PETRA   Mom...

ANGELA   You're his sister.

PETRA   Mom...

ANGELA   I wish I had a sister.

PETRA   You do.

ANGELA   ...No.

ACT TWO, SCENE FOUR

A coffee shop. Enter BERNARD and CLAY. They are wearing dog collars. LEGION and MAMMON are leading them in on leashes.

BERNARD   This is ridiculous.

CLAY   A coffee shop?

BERNARD   Petra wanted to meet somewhere neutral.

CLAY   May be a bit difficult to destroy her in a public place.

BERNARD   I don't want to talk to Petra. Whatever it is, I don't want to talk about it. Petra is so...

CLAY   Just remember who's running the show. We're in control here. We give the orders.

BERNARD   *(calling waiter)* Two coffees, please!

CLAY   How shall we destroy her?

PETRA   *(entering)* Clay, I'm here to talk to my brother. Remove yourself.

CLAY   Remove myse...I will not be told what to do by the likes of you. I have my dignity.

BERNARD   I can handle this, Clay.

PETRA	Handle what?
CLAY	We've come to destroy you.
PETRA	How?
CLAY	How?
BERNARD	Clay...
CLAY	What?
BERNARD	I can handle...
PETRA	Clay, get out.
CLAY	Out?
BERNARD	Clay...
PETRA	Away.
CLAY	I'm not going anywh...

> MAMMON tightens the leash and drags CLAY offstage.
>
> BERNARD is still being held on a leash.

PETRA	So now you plan to destroy me.
BERNARD	Look...

PETRA	My brother.
BERNARD	Don't overreact.
PETRA	She's using her little minions to do her dirty work now.
BERNARD	I'm not a minion.
PETRA	You're a trained poodle.
BERNARD	I resent that.
PETRA	You and Clay both.
BERNARD	Clay is special in his own way.
PETRA	He's completely manipulated. Just like you are.
BERNARD	Why don't you just give Auntie Francis a chance?
PETRA	I've given her twenty-one years of chances.
BERNARD	You don't even know her. Not like I do.
PETRA	You have no idea who she is.
BERNARD	Living with her is like a carnival ride. It's liberating.
PETRA	Liberating.
BERNARD	I'm free.
PETRA	From what?

BERNARD   From...

PETRA   What's so great about Auntie Francis?

BERNARD   She gives me free room and board.

PETRA   And?

BERNARD   She feeds me succulent meals.

PETRA   And?

BERNARD   She knows how to have a good time.

PETRA   And?

BERNARD   She parted the Red Sea.

PETRA   Auntie Francis did not part the Red Sea. That was Moses.

BERNARD   But if she wanted to part the Red Sea...

PETRA   You have a diseased mind.

BERNARD   If you would just...

PETRA   What? If I would just what? Join your commune in the basement where I can be pampered like a baby's butt and spoiled like expired yogurt?

BERNARD   Petra...

PETRA   After what she did to Mom?

BERNARD   Petra...

PETRA   I will not sell my mother for thirty pieces of silver.

BERNARD   There's freedom in the basement.

PETRA   Why would you want me to be free? You came here to destroy me. Clay said so.

BERNARD   Stop confusing me.

PETRA   How can I be confusing you? I'm the only one around here who makes any sense.

BERNARD   What is it that you want?

PETRA   A brother.

BERNARD   Yeah? Well I want a sister, but we can't always have what we want.

PETRA   Bernard...

BERNARD   Why are we here?

PETRA   I wanted to explain why I'm cutting Auntie Francis off.

BERNARD   Because you hate her.

PETRA   She's killing herself and all you do is coddle her.

BERNARD   Who cares if you cut her off? You're the only one. It isn't going to make a difference unless everyone is in it with you. You're alone, Petra. So why don't you save face, heh?

PETRA   Come home.

BERNARD   What the...No way. Auntie Francis needs me.

PETRA   Mom needs you.

BERNARD   I know my place. I...

PETRA   Do you realize that Mom is at home, groping a plush toy because she thinks her son has deserted her?

BERNARD   I can't go back there.

PETRA   Why?

BERNARD   Do you think it's easy for me to...When Mom is in so much...Do you think it's easy for me to watch?

PETRA   Who said anything about easy?

ACT TWO, SCENE FIVE

FRANCIS is in blackness, surrounded by LEGION and MAMMON, who are skulking around her.

FRANCIS   This is so easy. The world topples with a flick of my finger. Lives crumble in my fist. All I have to do is snap my fingers and poof! All my little disciples come running like confused termites. This isn't a puppet show anymore. I know what God knows. *(to MAMMON)* Garcon! My beverage!

MAMMON teases FRANCIS with a bottle of rum.

FRANCIS   Are you going to give me that or not?...What the...Give it...Son of a...

LEGION and MAMMON are amused.

FRANCIS   That's mine! I need it! The agony! Dizzy! I'm going to puke!

LEGION and MAMMON pin FRANCIS to the floor.

FRANCIS   We were supposed to be in this together. You promised...Ow!...You promised me! Ow! for the love of...Listen to me. I am still in control!

MAMMON spits on her.

FRANCIS   Lying son of a…At least give me a little to make the pain go away.

                                    They pull her by the hair.

FRANCIS   The pain, the pain, the pain, the pain, the pain. Just a drop. One frigging drop, for the love of… How could you be so cruel?

                                    They pull harder on her hair.

FRANCIS   I'm your bitch.

                                    LEGION and MAMMON point. The lights go up to reveal BERNARD, who is hurrying to put his coat on. LEGION and MAMMON slink away.

FRANCIS   Where do you think you're going?

BERNARD   I talked to Petra today. I'm needed at home.

FRANCIS   This is home.

BERNARD   I'll only be an hour. Maybe two. Mom's sick again and…

FRANCIS   I need you.

BERNARD   I know. I'm coming back. It's just…

FRANCIS   You can't leave me here. Not alone.

BERNARD   You'll be okay. But Mom's in really bad shape.

FRANCIS   I can't let you do this.

BERNARD   She's my mother.

FRANCIS slaps BERNARD.

FRANCIS   Don't ever let me hear those words come out of your mouth.

BERNARD   Yes, Auntie Francis. *(FRANCIS grabs BERNARD by the scruff of the neck)* Yes...Mom.

Fade out.

Fade in BERNARD. He is alone in blackness.

BERNARD   Um...I had this dream? I don't dream often, and when I do, I don't really remember much, but this dream...it scared me, I think. I was a soldier, fighting in a war. I don't remember what I was fighting for. The battlefield was covered with this black haze. Probably from gun smoke or something. The point is, I couldn't see. But I could hear screaming. Lots of it. I could hear Petra, Mom and Auntie Francis all screaming for me to help them, but I couldn't find them. There was that black haze. I realized that in order to save them, I had to ward off the enemy somehow. So I trudged through the battlefield, coughing. My eyes stung. The mud was swallowing my feet. I could see soldiers charging at me, but their uniforms were covered in filth and blood. I couldn't figure out who the enemy was. I could have easily mistaken one for a comrade. Then Cousin Clay suddenly materialized in the middle of the chaos. He was dressed like a pimp and counting fivers. It made sense at the time. Anyway, I didn't have much time, so I knew that I would only be able to rescue one person...Mom, Petra or Auntie Francis. I felt tugged on every side. I love my mom. I need my aunt. And Petra...she's my big sister. What in the world was I supposed to do? I couldn't see where I was going and I didn't know who the enemy was. You know, other guys my age are out playing hockey with their buddies or taking a cute girl to the matinee. Why do I have to make decisions like this? I'm only eighteen years old. I'm too young to be in a war.

Fade out BERNARD.

Fade in FRANCIS on the opposite side of the stage. She is talking to a bottle of rum.

FRANCIS   Are you the only friend I have? You're a pretty lousy friend. Take, take, take, that's what you do. I gave you my soul and all you do is take from me. But I love you anyway. Do you love me back? Of course not. Why should you? You piece of crap. You know, Mother used to always say that you can't help who you fall in love with. I don't know why I love you. Just remember that I don't *need* you. Nope. That would be pathetic. I *need* no one. I just *want* you. I want you bad. I could drop kick you out of my life at any time, but I don't *want* to... Seriously... Would you talk to me already? Jeez! Some friend.

Fade out FRANCIS.

ACT TWO, SCENE SIX

ANGELA'S kitchen. ANGELA is baking and PETRA is studying at the kitchen table.

PETRA   You're overdoing it, Mom. Please go lie down.

ANGELA   Francis is going to be so surprised!

PETRA   She won't be expecting it, I assure you. Here you are, after all, feeding the hand that bites you.

ANGELA   I shall be a vessel through which blessings flow.

PETRA   And Auntie Francis shall be a vessel through which rum flows.

ANGELA   I promised I'd look after Francis. I'm her big sister and I promised. It's my responsibility to meet her needs.

PETRA   She doesn't need a chocolate cake, Mom. She needs to be put in a de-tox centre.

ANGELA   Love is like a chocolate cake.

PETRA   Mom, love is not like a chocolate cake.

ANGELA   It is written, "Love is likened unto a chocolate cake."

PETRA   Leave it to Mom to turn chocolate cake into a parable.

ANGELA   Would you like me to explain why love is like a chocolate cake?

PETRA   What is a chocolate cake going to do for Auntie Francis? Absorb all the alcohol in her bloodstream?

ANGELA   I poured love into this springform pan, and Francis will change if I...

PETRA   You're worming your hook for more abuse.

ANGELA   At least I'm doing something for her. You're just hiding here with your snout in a textbook.

PETRA   I'm not the one who's hiding.

ANGELA   Are you hoping that if we all leave Francis by herself that we'll eventually find her stinking corpse fermenting in a puddle of whiskey?

PETRA   Suicide is not an Olympic sport, Mom. Francis does not need a cheering section.

ANGELA   I am bringing this cake to Francis so that I might be a beacon. Come, and be a beacon with me.

PETRA   I'm not going anywhere. You know where I stand on this issue.

ANGELA   There will be no issues in this house. You're coming with me.

PETRA   I've made a decision and...

ANGELA   I'm the mommy.

PETRA   You're not strong enough to take another blow.

ANGELA   I'm trying to have a sister.

PETRA   I'm trying to...

ANGELA   Get your coat.

PETRA   I'm trying to...

ANGELA   Auntie's waiting.

PETRA   I'm trying to...

ANGELA   *(cringing in pain)* Petra...

PETRA   You're not going anywhere alone.

ACT TWO, SCENE SEVEN

FRANCIS's kitchen. FRANCIS, BERNARD and CLAY are standing around an object which is covered with a sheet. CLAY pulls the sheet off.

CLAY   Tah-dah!

FRANCIS   It's...it's...

CLAY   It's a graven image of Auntie F. No home should be without one. Serves multiple purposes. One can gape at it fondly or bow down and worship. Do you like?

FRANCIS   My boy.

CLAY   It really is a staggering likeness. I thought it might be fun to gather around it each morning as we recite the prayer of St. Francis. Incense anyone?

FRANCIS   How fun!

CLAY   Let us all join hands now and meditate on the wonders of our sainted aunt. Let us ponder, if you will, the blessings Auntie F has bestowed upon us. Go ahead, ponder.

FRANCIS   Will you join us, Bernard?

BERNARD   I guess.

FRANCIS   My boy.

CLAY   Shall I slaughter a goat and present it to you as a burnt offering?

FRANCIS   No need. The graven image is more than enough for today.

                                    Enter ANGELA and PETRA.. PETRA coughs from the cigarette smoke. LEGION and MAMMON stand behind FRANCIS. Every movement and gesture FRANCIS makes, LEGION and MAMMON make simultaneously behind her as though they are puppet masters.

ANGELA   Where's my sweet, little sister?

FRANCIS   If it isn't the do-gooder and her lamb without blemish.

PETRA   It's smoky. I'll wait in the car.

FRANCIS   No need. When I lit a cigarette in my own home, I didn't realize the Christ child would be paying me a visit.

ANGELA   I brought a chocolate cake.

PETRA   I don't approve.

BERNARD   You don't approve of anything.

FRANCIS   Interesting, you should show your face here, Petra.

	After voicing your disapproval of my lifestyle. There's a name for people like you. It starts with the letter H.
PETRA	I only came in case Mom collapsed on the way here. I'll make myself scarce as soon as Mom gives you this here cake of love.
FRANCIS	A cake, Angela? A cake? I don't want a cake.
ANGELA	Why?
FRANCIS	Did you bring this because I'm your sister or because I'm your project? I don't need a sister.
ANGELA	Why?
FRANCIS	Everything I need is in my basement. My loving nephews and my lewd lovers in the wine cellar.
ANGELA	Why?
FRANCIS	Bet that looks really good on you, doesn't it, Perfect Petra? Bet you feel really good about yourself when Auntie Francis sins.
PETRA	Mom, let's go home.
ANGELA	Why?
PETRA	Mom?
ANGELA	Why, Francis? Why?

FRANCIS   Did you take pain killers?

ANGELA   Why can't I have a sister? Why was I alone? Why did you let him…

FRANCIS   Why are you making no sense?

ANGELA   When we were kids…

FRANCIS   What are you getting at?

ANGELA   When Dad hit me…

FRANCIS   Why would you bring this up now?

ANGELA   When he beat me with a rope in the basement. When he broke my nose.

FRANCIS   I don't need this.

ANGELA   Why didn't you do anything?

FRANCIS   I did do something.

ANGELA   What did you do?

FRANCIS   I watched.

CLAY   She has a point. Watching is technically doing something.

ANGELA   Why did you let him…

FRANCIS	I was five! Give me a break, will you?
ANGELA	Francis...
FRANCIS	Like there's a whole lot a five year old can do.
ANGELA	I still have scars.
FRANCIS	I need a drink.
ANGELA	Have some cake?
FRANCIS	Why do you keep trying to feed me? I eat like a queen. I don't need your charity.
ANGELA	But...
FRANCIS	And I don't need a sister. If I was Dad, I would have hit you myself.
PETRA	Are you possessed?
ANGELA	No, Petra. She's right. I deserve...
PETRA	Francis...
FRANCIS	*Auntie* Francis.
PETRA	My mother is a model human being. I don't think you realize how lucky you are.
FRANCIS	Just what I need. A sister who is a model human being. I'm sure the cake is perfect too. Probably fell from

heaven like manna in the desert! Flowing with milk and honey, no doubt.

PETRA   Look, just because you're screwed up, doesn't mean...

FRANCIS   What do you know? Do you even know what suffering is? Grief? Despair?

PETRA   As a matter of fact...

FRANCIS   I'll bet your exams are real hard. What a tumultuous life you must have.

PETRA   My mother is suffering.

FRANCIS   Get the hell out of my house!

BERNARD   What about the cake?

ANGELA   No worries. I'm sure I can find some nice lepers who might be hungry. Excuse me.

PETRA   Wait, Mom.

FRANCIS   Get out of here, Angela. And take your flipping cake with you. I'm sick of all those bloody, angel voices singing requiems every time you walk into a room. Go find someone who gives a damn, you miserable piece of sh...

> PETRA pounces, in an attempt to attack FRANCIS.
>
> LEGION and MAMMON stand in

the way. PETRA wrestles with LEGION and MAMMON on the floor while the others watch, confused.

PETRA   I've had enough of...you take that back, you lousy drunk...I want my family back, you...why I oughta'...Coward!...Lying piece of...Arg!...Enough! Do you hear me? Enough!

BERNARD   Who's Petra wrestling with?

CLAY   She's mad.

ANGELA   Petra, dear, is something troubling you?

PETRA   Get off of me! Are you deaf? You can't break me! You can't! I'm stronger! Get off! Boof! Arg! You can't hurt me anymore! God help me!

LEGION and MAMMON stop abruptly and scurry offstage. There is a pause as PETRA catches her breath.

FRANCIS   You're weird.

PETRA   I want to go home.

BERNARD   You're the only one who doesn't want to stay. It's a shame too.

PETRA   The shame is that Auntie Francis is going to die.

CLAY   At least we'll be left in her will.

PETRA   What?

CLAY   You had your chance. Too bad you can't invest principles into Equity Funds.

PETRA   You slimy, little...You know, the way Auntie Francis splurges, she's liable to die broke and alone. And you'll be left with dick.

CLAY   Dick? Who's Dick? Do we have to share our inheritance with him?

FRANCIS   Petra, your proverbial bosh is making me ill. I need a cigarette.

PETRA   I don't think that's such a good idea.

FRANCIS   Preach me a sermon.

PETRA   No, seriously...

BERNARD   She's an adult.

CLAY   This is her house.

ANGELA   Show Auntie some love.

PETRA   I wouldn't light that cigarette if I were you.

FRANCIS   You're *not* me. We all know *you've* never lit a cigarette. *You've* never tasted alcohol. And God forbid you should ever entertain the thought of fraternizing with sinners.

PETRA But...

FRANCIS Leave me alone and let me go to hell.

PETRA But Auntie Francis, you're so full of alcohol, an open flame may cause an explosion.

FRANCIS Why don't you go find some water and walk on it?

PETRA Auntie Fr...

> *FRANCIS lights her cigarette.*
> *FRANCIS explodes.*

PETRA Would you look at that? Auntie Francis just exploded. Nobody ever listens to me.

Finis

www.ingramcontent.com/pod-product-compliance
Lightning Source LLC
Chambersburg PA
CBHW021248170626
46808CB00011BA/2947